13664

E
Er

Eriksson, Eve
"Victory for
Rosalie"
short we...

D0894898

DATE DUE

AUG 6 1986	APR 29 1990	
JAN 17 1987	AUG 25 1990	
MAR 7 - 1987	OCT 30 1991	DISCARDED
JUL 25 1987	JUL 1 - 1992	
AUG 17 1987	JUL 25 1992	
SEP 16 1987	DEC 18 '93	
JAN 30 1988	SEP 9 '96	
FEB 8 - 1988	AUG 04 1999	
APR 9 - 1988	JUN 20 2001	
MAY 7 - 1988	JAN. 01 2003	
JUN 8 - 1988	DISCARDED	
JUL 30 1988		

DISCARDED

One Short Week

"Victor and Rosalie"
in
One Short Week

Eva Eriksson

Carolrhoda Books, Inc./Minneapolis

This edition first published 1985 by Carolrhoda Books, Inc.
Original edition published 1978 by Tidens Förlag, Stockholm, Sweden,
under the title OM EN LITEN VECKA ©1978 by Eva Eriksson
Translated from the Swedish by Barbro Eriksson Roehrdanz
Adapted by Carolrhoda Books, Inc.

Manufactured in the United States of America

LIBRARY OF CONGRESS CATALOGING IN PUBLICATION DATA

Eriksson, Eva.
  One short week.

  (Victor and Rosalie)
  Translation of: Om en liten vecka.
  Summary: Bored and having no one to play with,
Rosalie randomly dials the telephone and reaches
Victor who invites her to a birthday party.
  1. Children's stories, Swedish. [1. Boredom—Fiction.
2. Parties—Fiction] I. Title. II. Series: Eriksson,
Eva. Victor and Rosalie.
PZ7.E7259On 1985   [E]   84-17644
ISBN 0-87614-234-X (lib. bdg.)

1 2 3 4 5 6 7 8 9 10 93 92 91 90 89 88 87 86 85

/3 6 6 4

One Short Week

Rosalie had no one to play with. She was bored.

Her little brother, Martin, was too little.
He didn't know how to play.
He didn't even know how to eat
because he didn't have any teeth yet.
He only knew how to drink.
"Drink this!" Rosalie told him.
"Drink this and grow up
so that we can play together."

But Martin grew so slowly.
To tell the truth,
he burped a lot more than he grew.
Rosalie sighed.
"It's certainly not going to be this week
that we play together."

Then Rosalie made a discovery! A tiny ghost
lived under the dresser. He had lost his voice.
He couldn't scare anyone anymore,
so now he was bored, just like Rosalie.

"Look what I've found!" said Rosalie.
"A tiny little bored ghost!"

But Mama and Papa paid no attention.
They just talked and talked and talked.

Maybe Martin likes ghosts, thought Rosalie.
But Martin just wanted to chew.
He snatched the ghost in his toothless mouth.

"You've killed the ghost!" cried Rosalie.
"I'm going to call the police!
Just you wait!"
Rosalie dialed all kinds of numbers—
eights and sevens and zeros and lots more.

"My baby brother has eaten my sweet little ghost,"
she whispered into the telephone.
"Come and get him right away, please."

But the man who answered the telephone
was not a policeman.
He wasn't interested in little brothers who ate ghosts.
He was having his own problems with a moose.

Rosalie dialed some more numbers.
This time a boy answered. His name was Victor,
and he lived at 27 Blecking Avenue.
He knew all about babies
and not having anyone to play with
and feeling bored.

"Come to my birthday party!" said Victor.
"It's only one short week away."

The next day Rosalie drew a picture of herself.
It was a present for Victor.

Then she made a bow to put on her hat.
"It's not easy to make bows," she said to herself.
"It's downright difficult, that's what."

In fact, the bow looked better on Rosalie's dress.
Then she was ready.
There was nothing left to do but wait.
"That's enough!" said Rosalie at 2 o'clock.
"I'm sure that one short week has passed by now."

"I'm going to Victor's right now."
Rosalie set out.
She was sure she could find Victor's street.

She had only gone around the corner
when she met a lady.
The lady thought that Rosalie was lost.
"Where do you live, little girl?" she asked.

Rosalie told her.
She didn't have time to say more.
The lady had already brought her back
in front of her house.

"I'll never get to Victor's party this way,"
said Rosalie, and she screamed so hard
that all of her teeth showed.

A man came running.
He didn't have time to open his mouth
before Rosalie said, "27 Blecking Avenue."
The man took her there right away.

That's how Rosalie finally got to Victor's house.
"I'm glad you came right away," Victor told her.
"It's silly to have to wait for days and days.
We'll start the party right now."

Rosalie and Victor played for hours and hours, one hundred hours at least. Victor's mother telephoned Rosalie's parents, and they came to Victor's house too. But Victor and Rosalie didn't stop playing.

And when all the mothers and fathers and babies
had fallen asleep, Victor and Rosalie
were still playing.

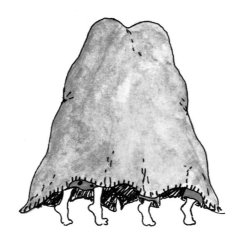

They played all night long
without making a sound,
and none of the mothers or fathers or babies
woke up even once.

Eva Eriksson

About the Author

Eva Eriksson was born and grew up in the southern Swedish town of Halmstad. From there she went to Stockholm where she completed her studies in art. Ms. Eriksson's career as an author and illustrator began soon after the birth of her son, Olle, in 1973. Some of the stories she then wrote for and about him later became the basis for her four books about Victor and Rosalie. Ms. Eriksson's many books for children have received wide international recognition. In 1981 she won the Elsa Beskow Plaquette for illustration and the prestigious Heffalump, awarded annually by the Swedish newspaper *Expressen* for the best children's book of the year.

Ms. Eriksson currently lives outside of Stockholm with her husband and their two children.